Typhon and the Winds of Destruction

HEROES IN TRAINING

Typhon and the Winds of Destruction

Joan Holub and Suzanne Williams

Aladdin

NEW YORK   LONDON   TORONTO   SYDNEY   NEW DELHI

This book is a work of fiction. Any references to historical events, real people,
or real places are used fictitiously. Other names, characters, places, and events are
products of the authors' imagination, and any resemblance to actual events
or places or persons, living or dead, is entirely coincidental.

ALADDIN

An imprint of Simon & Schuster Children's Publishing Division
1230 Avenue of the Americas, New York, NY 10020
First Aladdin paperback edition December 2013
Text copyright © 2013 by Joan Holub and Suzanne Williams
Illustrations copyright © 2013 by Craig Phillips
All rights reserved, including the right of reproduction
in whole or in part in any form.
ALADDIN is a trademark of Simon & Schuster, Inc.,
and related logo is a registered trademark of Simon & Schuster, Inc.
Also available in an Aladdin hardcover edition.
For information about special discounts for bulk purchases,
please contact Simon & Schuster Special Sales
at 1-866-506-1949 or business@simonandschuster.com.
The Simon & Schuster Speakers Bureau can bring authors to your live event.
For more information or to book an event,
contact the Simon & Schuster Speakers Bureau at 1-866-248-3049
or visit our website at www.simonspeakers.com.
Cover designed by Karin Paprocki
Interior designed by Mike Rosamilia
The text of this book was set in Adobe Garamond Pro.
Manufactured in the United States of America 0816 OFF
2 4 6 8 10 9 7 5 3
Library of Congress Control Number 2013950783
ISBN 978-1-4424-8842-7 (pbk)
ISBN 978-1-4424-8844-1 (hc)
ISBN 978-1-4424-8843-4 (eBook)

⚡ Contents ⚡

Greetings,
Mortal Readers,

I am Pythia, the Oracle of Delphi, in Greece. I have the power to see the future. Hear my prophecy:

Ahead I see dancers lurking. Wait—make that *danger* lurking. (The future can be blurry, especially when my eyeglasses are foggy.)

Anyhoo, beware! Titan giants seek to rule all of Earth's domains—oceans, mountains, forests, and the depths of the Underwear. Oops— make that *Underworld*. Led by King Cronus, they are out to destroy us all!

Yet I foresee hope. A band of rightful rulers called Olympians will arise. Though their size and youth are no match for the Titans, they will be giant in heart, mind, and spirit. They await their leader—a very special boy. One who is destined to become king of the gods and ruler of the heavens.

If he is brave enough.

And if he and his friends work together as one. And if they can learn to use their new amazing flowers—um, amazing *powers*—in time to save the world!

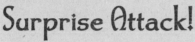

CHAPTER ONE

Surprise Attack!

Ouch!" ten-year-old Zeus yelled as a hot orange spark hit his shoulder.

"Sorry," said Hestia. "I'm trying to figure out how to control this thing."

She held up a long metal torch decorated with carvings. A bright flame danced in the shallow bowl at the top of the torch.

"Well, maybe you should try a little harder," Hera muttered under her breath.

Zeus knew that Hera was upset. Yesterday he and his five young Olympian friends had found the Olympic Torch and its eternal flame. Hera had hoped the magical object would be hers. But the magic only worked when Hestia held the torch.

Zeus tried changing the subject. "I think we'll get to that giant beanstalk in just a couple of hours."

He nodded into the distance. A tall green stalk with big leaves had sprouted up from the ground early that morning. The stalk had grown so tall that its top disappeared into the clouds. Pythia, the Oracle of Delphi, had sent them on a quest to find Magic Seeds, and the giant beanstalk looked like a good place to start.

Poseidon, whose eyes were the color of the ocean, rubbed his stomach. "If we find those Magic Seeds, I just might eat them," he said.

"We've been walking all morning, and we haven't eaten since last night."

"Hey! Is that a farmhouse?" said red-haired Demeter. She pointed into the distance. "Maybe we can get something to eat there."

Hera frowned. "Do we have to stop? We're not that far from the beanstalk now."

"Actually, I'm kind of hungry too," Hades admitted.

"It's not a bad idea to stop," Zeus reasoned. "We might need our strength to face . . . whatever's waiting for us at that stalk."

The other Olympians knew what he meant. Every time they went searching for a new magical object or a missing Olympian, they got into some kind of danger. Sometimes King Cronus of the Titans sent monsters to stop them. Or other Titans hurled fireballs at them, or tried to kidnap them, or worse.

Sure, the giant beanstalk looked like a harmless plant, but Zeus knew by now that anything could happen. And when it did, it would probably be bad.

Poseidon broke into a run. "Lunch, here I come!" he said, racing toward the farmhouse.

The others took off after him. When they got to the farmhouse, they saw a gray-haired farmer pulling weeds from a scraggly-looking vegetable patch.

"What are you kids doing all the way out here?" he asked.

Poseidon spoke up. "We're going to look for the Mag— *Oof!*"

Zeus had nudged him in the ribs. "We're on a journey," he explained. "And we're pretty hungry. We were wondering if you had any food to spare?"

The old man scratched his head. "Well, I lost

a lot of crops during the drought," he said. "But I do have plenty of eggs, thanks to the chickens, and some carrots."

"We'd be happy to do a few chores to repay you," Demeter said sweetly.

Charmed, the farmer smiled. "Well, isn't that nice. Let me go cook something up."

"I can light your hearth," Hestia offered, following him inside.

Zeus looked around the yard. Brown and white chickens scratched the dry earth. Two pigs slept peacefully in a pen. A pile of logs was stacked against the chicken coop.

"Let's make ourselves useful," Zeus said to the other Olympians. "I'll chop some wood." He took the dagger-size thunderbolt from his belt.

"Bolt, large!" he commanded. The dagger sizzled and sparked, and then expanded into a five-foot-long thunderbolt. With Bolt he could slice through a stack of logs like they were butter. He had found the magic thunderbolt at the temple at Delphi, before he had even met the others. It had helped get him through a lot of dangerous situations. But it was great at doing ordinary stuff too.

"I'll fill the troughs," Poseidon offered. He held up his three-pronged trident, which he had taken back from a Titan called Oceanus. That's when he'd discovered that he was the god of the sea and could control water. Poseidon pointed the trident at the pigs' wooden trough, and it instantly filled up with water.

"I'll clean out the pigpen!" Hades announced cheerfully, his dark eyes twinkling.

Demeter wrinkled her nose. "Yuck! Why do you look so happy about it?" she asked.

Hades took a deep breath. "Ahhh, that smell! I can't get enough of it. It's an Underworld thing."

Hera shook her head. "It's a *weird* thing."

"Hey, you're talking to the lord of the Underworld, you know," Hades reminded her.

"More like the lord of the pigpen," Hera shot back. She still looked upset over that torch.

"You okay, Hera?" Zeus asked. "You usually save your insults for me."

Demeter tugged the sleeve of Hera's tunic. "Let's go feed the chickens," she said.

Thanks to the magical objects (and Hades's love of smelly stuff), they finished the chores quickly. Then they took their seats at the large farmhouse table and dug into their lunch.

"You kids enjoy," the farmer said. "You certainly earned it."

He shuffled off into the other room, and Zeus nodded to Poseidon, who sat across the table.

"Don't go blabbing about the Magic Seeds," he warned Poseidon in a loud whisper. "If word gets around that we're looking for magic stuff, Cronus might find out and come looking for us."

"Oh. Right," Poseidon whispered back.

Demeter looked out the window at the farmer's fields. Most of the crops had withered and turned brown, thanks to a Titan named Hyperion. He had been hurling fireballs across the land, causing a terrible drought, until the Olympians had stopped him.

"Hyperion's drought really devastated the land," she remarked. "I hope we do find the Magic Seeds so that we can bring back the crops, like Pythia said."

"Well, I just hope the *right* person gets the seeds," Hera said, with a look at Hestia.

"What do you mean?" Hestia asked, her light brown eyes wide.

"Oh, nothing," Hera said, but her voice was

tight. "It's just that, you know, some of us have been doing these quests longer than others and still haven't gotten our magical objects. It doesn't seem fair."

Zeus felt kind of bad for Hera. "I don't think the magical objects are in a specific order as far as who they belong to. Maybe you just need to be patient."

Hera put down her fork. "We should get going. I'll wait outside."

She stomped out of the farmhouse, her long blond hair swaying down her back.

"Wow, she's about as happy as a fish in a net," Poseidon said.

Demeter spoke up. "Well, I don't blame her."

"How would you feel if you didn't have your trident yet?"

"Well, I don't think I would—"

"Aaaaaaaaahhh!"

A loud scream came from outside. Zeus jumped up from the table and and ran to push open the farmhouse door. He and the others rushed outside.

Three half-giants, who were as tall as trees, stood in front of the pigpen. The largest one grasped Hera in one beefy arm. She kicked and scratched, trying to get free.

"It's the Cronies!" Zeus yelled.

CHAPTER TWO

The Power of Six

Zeus reached for Bolt, but before he could release it—

An arrow made of fire hit the chest of the Crony holding Hera. Shrieking, he dropped her, and she ran to join the other Olympians.

Puzzled, Zeus looked over at Hestia, who stared at her torch in amazement.

"It's weird," she said. "I was just thinking

about using the torch to help Hera, and the fire arrow just . . . happened."

"Can you make it happen again?" Poseidon asked nervously.

Angry now, the three Cronies stomped toward the Olympians. Zeus knew them by the names he had given them based on what they looked like. Lion Tattoo, Blackbeard, and Double Chin all worked for King Cronus. Not long ago they had kidnapped Zeus and tried to eat him—but that was before Zeus had found his magical weapon.

"Bolt, large!" Zeus yelled, and the dagger transformed in his hand. He pointed it at Lion Tattoo.

Zap! A jagged wave of electricity shot from Bolt and hit Lion Tattoo smack in the middle of his armored breastplate. The big soldier went down, taking the other two Cronies with him.

The loud bellow of a battle cry echoed through-
out the farm.

"There's more of them!" Poseidon yelled as
the sound of stomping boots grew closer.

Zeus turned to see a line of Cronies charging
up from the back of the farmhouse. He counted
four on either side of the building.

Whoosh! An array of fire arrows flew at the
Cronies, but the half-giants barreled right
through them.

"It's time for a high five!" Hades cried.

Zeus held up Bolt, Hades held out his Helm
of Darkness, and Poseidon held out his trident.
The Helm made whoever wore it invisible.

Zeus nodded to Hestia. "The torch!"

She touched the torch to the other objects.
Hera and Demeter each added a hand. Instantly
the weapons all began to sizzle and glow with
tremendous power. A bright white light exploded

from them, blinding the stunned Cronies.

"Now!" Zeus yelled.

They broke apart and began to attack the Cronies all at once.

Whoosh! A mighty wave sprang from Poseidon's trident, knocking down a line of four Cronies.

Zap! A supercharged jolt of energy from Bolt hit Blackbeard and ricocheted off Lion Tattoo and Double Chin. This time the blast sent them flying, and they smacked into a stand of trees.

Boom! More fire arrows sprang from the torch and landed in the dry grass near the third group of Cronies. The grass exploded into flames, encircling the Cronies in a ring of red-hot fire.

"Run for it!" Poseidon yelled, racing off.

"Wait!" Hera cried. "We can't just leave the farm to burn."

Zeus knew she was right. That ring of fire would quickly spread.

"Poseidon, put out the fire," he called out. "I'll stay with you, and the others can run for it."

"No need," Hades said, slipping his helmet on. He immediately became invisible. "I'll distract them so Poseidon can get away."

"Sounds like a plan," Poseidon said, holding up his trident.

Zeus hated to leave his friends, but he knew that Hades and Poseidon could handle things. He and the girls raced off past the surprised farmer, who stood in his doorway with his mouth open.

"Thanks for lunch!" Zeus yelled as he ran.

Looking behind him, Zeus saw Poseidon wipe out the circle of fire with another giant wave. The third group of Cronies retreated into the woods as Poseidon took off at top speed after the other Olympians.

The five Olympians ran until they reached

a small grove of olive trees, and then came to a stop.

"We should wait here," Zeus said, panting. "Hades knows we're heading for the beanstalk. He'll find us."

"Sorry about those fire arrows back there," Hestia said. "But I think I'm figuring it out. I can make the flame from the torch jump anywhere I want. I just have to concentrate."

"That's okay," Zeus said. "I didn't know how to use Bolt when I first got it either."

Hestia smiled gratefully at Zeus. Out of the corner of one of his blue eyes, he saw Hera scowling at him and Hestia.

I hope the Magic Seeds turn out to be Hera's magical object, he thought. *She'll be impossible to live with if someone else gets them!*

Demeter walked up to one of the olive trees. It looked like it had done its best to survive the drought, but each branch held only a few thin green leaves and small white flowers.

"Poor thing," she said, gently touching the trunk with her hand. Instantly more leaves and branches sprouted on the nearest branch.

Zeus had seen Demeter do this kind of thing before. He wanted to ask her about it, but suddenly Hades appeared right in front of him, holding his helmet.

"So what do you call a Crony who tells lies?" he asked, grinning.

"I don't know. What?" Zeus asked.

"A phony Crony!" Hades replied, cracking up. "Good one, right?"

Hera shook her head. "So what happened back there?"

"Well, the rest of the Cronies were knocked out pretty good," Hades answered. "So I waited until the biggest one woke up, and then I started

talking loudly, like you guys were still there. I said that we were all heading east. So he told the other Cronies, and they totally went in the wrong direction."

He grinned again, pleased with himself.

"They'll soon figure out that they're on the wrong trail," Hera pointed out.

"Maybe not," said Hestia. She looked up into the sky, and then turned so she faced east. She closed her eyes, concentrating, and the flame in the torch began to dance.

"What did you do?" Zeus asked.

"I made a bunch of campfires out by the eastern hills so the Cronies will think it's us," she explained. "That should keep them busy for a while."

"Good thinking," said Zeus. "Now let's get moving before those Cronies figure things out and catch up to us!"

CHAPTER THREE

To Climb or Not to Climb

N
o Cronies on our trail yet," Hades reported a few hours later. He had donned his helmet again and scouted the trail behind them.

Hera pointed ahead. "Good thing, because we're almost there."

They could all get a clearer picture of the beanstalk now. Wide leaves grew from stems coming off the stalk, and it seemed to disappear into the clouds above.

Demeter's green eyes shone with excitement. "What an amazing plant!"

Zeus started to feel excited too. "Come on. Let's get there before the Cronies catch us," he said, breaking into a run.

The others followed, and soon they all reached the bottom of the stalk.

"Wow! That is one giant beanstalk!" Poseidon exclaimed.

Zeus looked up. The beanstalk was wider around than any tree he had ever seen. Its enormous green leaves cast shadows on the grass under his feet. He looked up, craning his neck, but he still couldn't see the top of the stalk.

"You can say that again," Zeus agreed.

"That is one giant beanstalk!" Poseidon repeated, which made Hestia giggle.

"It looks way taller than it did from back where we started," Hera remarked nervously.

Zeus pushed against the stalk. It was as hard as a tree trunk and didn't move at all. "It's sturdy," he reported. "Should be safe to climb."

Hera spun around to face Zeus. "What do you mean, *climb*?"

"Well, we're looking for Magic Seeds," Zeus replied. "If they're part of this beanstalk, they're probably in the bean pods or something."

He shaded his eyes and looked up again. "I don't see any pods down here, but they might be growing farther up."

"So let's chop it down!" Poseidon suggested. "You can use Bolt. One good whack, and boom! Magic Seeds."

Demeter ran between Zeus and the beanstalk. "Don't you dare!" she cried. "This beanstalk is a living thing. Chopping it down would be like . . . murder!"

"So are you saying that you murdered

those carrots we had for lunch today?" Hades asked.

"Well, no, but . . ." Demeter looked up at the stalk. "This is special, can't you see? It's probably the only one like it in the world. We can't just chop it down."

Poseidon sighed. "Oh, okay. If you say so."

"Isn't it more likely that some of the seeds have fallen to the ground?" Hera asked. "They might be buried in the dirt around here. We should dig."

Zeus shook his head. "I don't know. I just have a feeling that the seeds are up there somewhere," he said, pointing. Then he had a thought. He tugged on the leather cord that was around his neck. A smooth stone as big as his fist was strung on the cord.

"What do you think, Chip?" he asked the stone amulet.

As soon as he'd asked the question, an arrow

appeared on the stone—an arrow clearly pointing up. Zeus had found Chip in the temple at Delphi, where he had also found Bolt. Sometimes the stone talked to him in its own language, and at other times symbols appeared on it.

"Chip says the beans are up there," Zeus reported. "We definitely need to climb."

"Speak for yourself," Hera said, folding her arms across her chest. "I am staying right here."

Poseidon grinned. "You know what, Hera? I think maybe you're afraid of heights, just like I used to be afraid of water."

"That's ridiculous!" Hera protested, but Zeus could tell by her red face that Poseidon's guess was probably right.

"How about this," Zeus suggested. "Whoever wants to climb can come with me. If you don't want to climb, you can stay here and be on guard in case the Cronies find us."

"Fine," Hera said.

"I'd rather stay down here too," Hestia admitted.

"Me too," agreed Hades. "I'm more of an *Under*world guy than an *Above*world guy."

Demeter looked at Zeus. "I want to climb. I really want to see what's up there."

"I'll climb," Poseidon said. "It's way less boring than hanging out down here."

Zeus nodded. "Okay. Then Hera, Hestia, and Hades will stand guard." He grinned. "Hey, you guys are the three *H*s. *H*, like in—"

"Horrors! The Three Horrors!" Hades cried.

"Speak for yourself," Hera said.

Hestia spoke up shyly. "How about the Three Helpers?"

"Ugh!" Hera protested. "We are more than just helpers. It's got to be the Three Heroes. Remember, Pythia said we're heroes in training."

"Well, technically all six of us are heroes," Zeus declared. "So it's the Six Heroes."

"But that doesn't make sense," Hera argued. "We're the *three H*s. You said so yourself. So we can call ourselves the Three Heroes if we want to."

"Do I have to dump cold water on you guys?" Poseidon asked. "We need to get climbing before the Cronies find us."

"Right," Zeus agreed. He felt silly arguing with Hera, but she always seemed to get under his skin. "If the Cronies show up, Hestia and Hades, you can combine your objects and try to hold them off."

"Or maybe we can fool them again and try to throw them off track," Hestia suggested.

"And what am I supposed to do? Just sit here?" Hera asked, sounding annoyed.

Zeus looked down at Chip. The arrow

glowed a bright green color, which meant that Chip thought they should get moving too. Zeus reached up and grabbed the lowest leaf stem, which was as thick as a normal tree branch.

"Let's do this," Zeus said. "See you later, Three Hanger-Outers!"

"You mean the Three Heroes, Bolt Breath!" Hera insisted stubbornly.

This time Zeus didn't argue. He swung up onto the stem and began the long climb to the top of the beanstalk.

CHAPTER FOUR

Into the Clouds

Poseidon and Demeter scrambled up the beanstalk after Zeus. Luckily, the thick stalk had lots of bumps and crevices they could hold on to. The strong leaf stems were good for climbing too, and were about as wide as a Crony's arm. But the Olympians had a long, long way to go.

They kept climbing. Zeus could feel a chill in the air as they went higher. A little brown bird flew past his face and settled on a stem.

Chirp! Chirp!

Poseidon caught up to Zeus. "Hey, bird. Do you know how much farther we need to climb?" he asked it. The bird chirped and flew away.

"Nice try," Zeus said. "Did you really think it would answer you?"

Poseidon shrugged. "We're climbing a giant beanstalk, so a talking bird doesn't seem so crazy. Anyway, I'm getting pretty tired of climbing."

Zeus looked up.

"I still can't see the top," he said with a sigh. "It's nothing but clouds."

"Maybe there is no top," Poseidon suggested. "Maybe it just goes on . . . and on . . . and on . . ."

Demeter hoisted herself up onto a leaf stem.

"I think I see some blossoms up there," she announced. "Maybe we'll find some bean pods."

"I hope so," Zeus replied.

Demeter reached a blossom first, a white flower about as wide as she was tall.

"It's so pretty!" she cried, touching it gently. Then her eyes lit up. "I see a pod!"

She carefully walked along the stem, putting one foot in front of the other, like she was walking a tightrope. She didn't seem nervous at all to be up so high. When she reached the long green pod, she touched it. It automatically opened. Three shiny green beans, each the size of her head, were nestled inside.

"Could these be the Magic Seeds?" she asked excitedly.

"Let me ask Chip," Zeus replied. Steadying himself against the stalk with one hand, he held out the stone amulet with the other. A bright red *X* appeared on it.

"No," Zeus reported, and Demeter looked

disappointed. Then a green arrow appeared on Chip, pointing up. "We've got to keep climbing," Zeus said.

"I still think we should have just chopped this thing down," Poseidon muttered. Then he stepped ahead of Zeus and pulled himself up into the leafy canopy. He vanished into the green.

Zeus's arms started to feel the strain as he kept climbing. He pulled himself up to another stem, right next to a huge white flower bud.

"Boo!" The bud popped open, and Poseidon jumped out.

Startled, Zeus almost lost his footing. He quickly grabbed on to a leaf to steady himself.

Poseidon was cracking up.

"Not funny," Zeus said, still shaking. "I could have fallen!"

"Sorry," Poseidon said. "This climb is getting

kind of boring. I had to do something to liven things up."

Zeus climbed onto another stem. His head was surrounded by clouds. He reached through the cloud cover, grabbed the next stem overhead, and pulled himself up.

"Wow," he gasped. "Guys, I think this is it!"

The top of the stalk ended at what Zeus could only guess was some kind of island in the sky. He stepped out onto a field of grass with blades as tall as he was. But what really shocked him was the enormous house that loomed in front of him. The building was made of bricks of red clay and had a roof of rough wood shingles. The large green door had what appeared to be some kind of dragon carved into it.

"Squishy squids!" Poseidon cried out next to Zeus.

"That is a very big house," Demeter remarked.

"It is," agreed Zeus. "And whoever lives in it must be big. Really big."

"Do you think it's a Titan?" Poseidon asked nervously.

"Maybe," Zeus replied. "But this house is bigger than any Titan's house we've ever seen."

Demeter looked around. "I don't see any seeds lying around out here."

"Let's go into the house," said Zeus. "There's nothing else up here, so the seeds must be inside it."

"How are we supposed to open that door?" Poseidon asked.

"I don't think we'll need to," Zeus said. "Come on."

They walked through the tall grass until they reached the massive front door. The crack under the door looked almost large enough for them to crawl through.

Poseidon got on his knees. "I don't see any huge feet in there."

"Can you slide under?" asked Zeus.

Poseidon cautiously scooted forward. The top of his head bumped into the bottom of the door.

"Ow!" he cried. He slid back, rubbing his head.

"I'll fix things," Zeus said confidently. He whipped out his sizzling thunderbolt. "Large, Bolt!"

Once the bolt expanded, Zeus used it to shave off some of the wood at the bottom of the door. *Whack! Whack!*

"Try again," he suggested to Poseidon.

Poseidon pointed toward the crack with his trident. "After you."

Zeus ducked under the door, keeping Bolt extended just in case. He emerged into a huge, wide room filled with a giant table and chairs.

Each looked big enough to hold two Titans. Across the room was a massive bed—at least, that's what he thought it was. He couldn't tell for sure from way down on the floor. He didn't hear or see anyone who might live here, though.

"The coast is clear," he called to his friends.

Poseidon and Demeter joined him.

"What now?" Poseidon asked, looking around.

Zeus checked Chip for directions, but the stone was blank—and silent. "I guess we should look around," he replied. "There's no red *X* on my amulet, so maybe that means the seeds are here somewhere."

"It's going to take forever to search this place," Poseidon grumbled. "And we don't even know what we're— Aaaah!"

Zeus spun around and saw a huge, furry ball rolling toward Poseidon, who started poking at it with his trident.

"I think that's just a dust bunny," Demeter piped up.

Poseidon paused. "Oh." But he kept poking it. "Maybe it's an *evil* dust bunny!"

Zeus scanned the room. More dust bunnies dotted the floor, along with boulders that he realized were probably breadcrumbs. But no seeds.

"I think we're going to have to climb up high to get a better look," he announced. He nodded to one of the legs of the bed, a tall wooden post that was as big around as the leg of a Titan. "Let's try that."

They dodged more dust bunnies as they made their way toward the post. Carvings in the post allowed them to grab hold as they climbed. A few minutes later they tumbled out onto what looked and felt like a big, soft field.

"It's a bed," Poseidon realized.

"With a cute bedspread," Demeter remarked.

"See? It's got pictures of little mice on it. Maybe whoever lives here isn't a big, scary monster, after all."

Suddenly Chip began to talk. *"Anger-dip! Anger-dip!"*

By now Zeus knew the amulet's language well. Chip spoke Chip Latin, which was kind of like Pig Latin, only you moved the first letter of each word to the end of the word and added "ip."

"Chip says there's danger!" Zeus translated.

Creeeaaaaak! The sound of the door opening— the door they'd crawled under only minutes before—made Zeus jump. "Quick, hide!" he whispered.

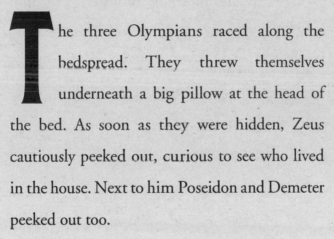

CHAPTER FIVE

Typhon

The three Olympians raced along the bedspread. They threw themselves underneath a big pillow at the head of the bed. As soon as they were hidden, Zeus cautiously peeked out, curious to see who lived in the house. Next to him Poseidon and Demeter peeked out too.

"Whoa!" Poseidon exclaimed, and Zeus clapped a hand over Poseidon's mouth.

The giant entering the room had a craggy face with dark eyes and a shaggy black beard. His chest and arms were muscled and strong. Two wings covered with shiny black feathers grew from his back. Instead of legs the lower half of his body was made up of a tangle of giant living snakes. They wiggled back and forth as he slithered across the floor into the house.

"That is definitely a monster. Probably another of Cronus's Creatures of Chaos!" Zeus whispered.

The giant paused and sniffed the air. His huge nostrils flared. Then he began to chant.

> *"Fee, fi, fo, fun.*
> *I smell the blood of an Olympian.*
> *Be he alive or even half-dead,*
> *I'll gobble him down until I'm fed."*

The three Olympians retreated farther under the pillow.

"Uh-oh! I think he smells us," Zeus hissed, hoping the pillow would muffle his words.

The giant looked around the room. "Come out, come out, wherever you aaaaaaare!" he called. His last word sounded like the bleating of a goat.

"Don't move," Demeter whispered.

Zeus didn't think he could have moved even if he'd wanted to. He was frozen with terror.

His heart pounded as the giant began to slither toward the bed. Had he heard them? Zeus tightly gripped Bolt, and Poseidon held his trident in front of him. But the giant only tossed his green cloak onto the bed. Then he changed direction.

He slithered up to the big wooden table and

picked up a giant-size stone sugar bowl. He lifted
its lid and grinned.

"There you are, my friend. I'd almost forgot-
ten where I put you last! *Awk! Awk! Awk!*" His
laugh sounded more like the cackling of a bird
than a real laugh. Then he reached into the bowl
and plucked out a boy with spiky hair as golden
as Hera's.

"He's our size!" Zeus exclaimed in a whisper.

Shiny crystals that looked like sugar clung to
the boy's clothes. Zeus could see that the boy
was quaking with fear. But that didn't stop him
from confronting the giant.

"Put me down, Typhon, you big bag of wind!
I don't like you, and you are *NOT* my friend!"
the boy shouted.

"Did he just rhyme on purpose?" Demeter
wondered quietly.

The giant chuckled, sounding something like

a frog croaking. He dangled the boy from his fingers.

"Aw, come on, little Olympian," he said in his loud, gruff voice. "I won't really eat you. Not as long as you continue to please me with your music, anyway." The giant grinned wickedly and let out a wolflike howl.

Zeus turned to his friends, puzzled. "Did I hear right? Did that Typhon guy just call that kid an Olympian?" he whispered. Pythia had *said* that they might find more Olympians on their new quest. Looked like she was right.

"And he's a musician, too," Demeter added.

Poseidon's hand tightened on his trident, and Zeus knew what his friend was thinking. That they had to rescue this boy.

Of course they did. But first Zeus had to figure out what was up with this monster. He had a beastly body, snakes for legs, and wings, and he made strange animal sounds. Who knew what dastardly things Typhon could do.

"Not yet," Zeus told Poseidon. "We need to think carefully before we make our move."

CHAPTER SIX

The Monster's Lullaby

Poseidon scowled, seeming impatient to rescue the boy. But Zeus knew it was smart to take care. They watched, hidden by the pillow, to see what the giant would do next.

Typhon placed the boy on the table and took a seat. He ripped off a hunk of bread from a loaf before him. Then he cut a chunk of cheese to go with it. He banged his fist on the table.

"Play!" he commanded in a voice like a lion's roar.

Zeus noticed that the boy had a sack slung over his shoulder. He opened the sack and took out a beautiful stringed instrument that was sort of like a portable harp—a lyre. The boy cradled the golden lyre in his arms and began to strum.

Beautiful music flowed from the lyre, filling the giant's house. Zeus had never heard anything like it before. It was like the sound of a waterfall cascading into a pool below, or the sighing of the wind in the trees, or the trilling of the birds in spring. Or maybe it sounded like all those things at once.

Zeus glanced at Poseidon and Demeter. They both had dreamy expressions on their faces as they listened.

As Typhon stuffed bread and cheese into his

giant mouth, the spiky-haired boy began singing. Sunlight glinted off the crystals stuck to his tunic as he belted out his song:

"Oh, Typhon is great and powerful.
No other giant is better.
And anyone who says otherwise,
He'll eat with bread and butter.

He roars with the strength of a lion,
A sound that makes others grow pale.
His wings are as strong as an eagle's,
And his belly's as big as a whale."

The giant frowned. "Belly as big as a whale? Are you saying I'm fat?"

"Oh no, sir," the boy said innocently. "The whale is the greatest creature in the sea. It's a compliment."

The giant nodded, satisfied. Under the pillow

the three Olympians tried not to laugh out loud.
This boy was pretty clever.

He began another verse.

"Typhon burns with the flame of a dragon.
All who see him shiver with dread.
He walks with the power of the serpent,
And his heart is as hard as his head."

Typhon frowned again. "A hard head? What
do you mean by that?"

"Only that no arrow can pierce it, oh great
Typhon," the boy replied with a little bow.

Once again the giant seemed satisfied, and
the Olympians struggled to stop their giggles.
The boy continued his song.

"Oh, Typhon is great and powerful,
And so is his mighty stench—"

"Aaaaachooooooooooo!" Poseidon sneezed so loudly that he drowned out the boy's singing.

Zeus quickly clapped a hand over Poseidon's mouth in case he had another sneeze coming.

"What was that?" the giant asked, half-rising from his chair.

"I don't know," the boy replied, a curious look on his face. "Probably nothing. Want me to finish the song?"

The giant settled back down. "Continue!"

Zeus glared at Poseidon. "No more sneezing!"

Poseidon pushed Zeus's hand away and whispered, "I can't help it! I think I'm allergic to the feathers in the pillow. *Aa . . . aa . . .*"

Quickly Demeter pinched Poseidon's nose with her fingers. "Try to hold it in," she urged him.

The boy strummed the lyre again.

"Oh, Typhon is great and powerful.

His arms are as thick as tree trunks.

His breath is as strong as the North Wind,

And it smells just as bad as ten skunks."

Typhon looked really angry this time. "Skunks?" he roared.

"The skunk's greatest weapon is his stench," the boy explained. "Even the strongest predator fears the skunk. Just as all creatures fear you, oh great Typhon."

"As they should!" the giant agreed. "Well done!" He pounded the table with his fist, and then several things happened at once.

"Aaaaachoooooo!" Poseidon sneezed so strongly that Demeter's fingers lost their grip.

Braaaaaaaaaap! Typhon let out a loud, long burp, covering up the sound of the sneeze. As his mouth opened wide, a stream of hot orange flame shot from it. The musical boy had to jump out of the way. He tumbled onto his back on the table.

Zeus remembered the boy's song. *Typhon burns with the flame of a dragon.* . . . Is that what this Creature of Chaos was? Some kind of half-giant, half-dragon?

The boy leaped to his feet. "You should warn me before you do that!" he scolded Typhon. "You'll fry me like an egg!"

"Then you shall be all the more delicious if I decide to eat you," Typhon replied. He banged the table again. "Play another one."

The boy nodded and strummed the lyre again. This time the music was slow and soothing, like a lullaby. Next to Zeus, Demeter let out a small sigh.

"He seems very sweet," she whispered. "And not just because he's covered in sugar."

The boy began to sing again.

"Close your eyes and go to sleep.
Lose yourself in slumber deep.
Count little mice inside your head,
And swallow them up until they're dead."

Demeter grimaced, and Zeus looked at the
pattern of mice on the blanket.

Well, Typhon is partly made of snakes, and snakes
love mice, so I guess that makes sense, he reasoned.

The boy sang another verse, and this one was
the meanest yet. But the pleasant tune of the lullaby kept the giant calm.

"Close your eyes, you big old oaf.
Your breath smells like moldy meat loaf.
You're mean and cruel, you bag of air.
I hope you fall right off your chair."

Luckily for the boy, the giant was sound asleep and soon began to snore. When the first snore escaped his hairy nostrils, a whirlwind escaped. It blew the loaf of bread off the table, and it wooshed the dust bunnies around on the floor.

"He really *is* a big bag of wind!" Poseidon exclaimed.

Zzzzzzzzzz.

The giant exhaled again, and this time the wind knocked over one of the chairs.

"He's going to destroy this place if he doesn't stop," Demeter observed worriedly.

Zzzzzzzzzz.

This time the snore sent the boy and his lyre flying right off the table! The Olympian friends watched in alarm as the whirlwind tossed him about. At last he landed with a plop, safely and softly, on the gigantic bed. His head barely

missed the pillow under which the Olympians were hiding!

"Now!" Zeus whispered to Poseidon and Demeter. They crept out from under the pillow and gathered around the boy, who slowly sat up, looking dazed. His eyes widened in surprise when he saw the Olympians.

"Who are you? What do you do?" the rhyming boy demanded.

CHAPTER SEVEN

Apollo's Tale

ong story," Zeus said. "But don't worry. We're on your side. We'll tell you more while we're getting out of here. I mean, Typhon won't sleep forever." He nodded toward the napping giant.

"But I don't understand," the boy said. "Did Typhon capture you, too, while he was outside?"

"No, we came here on our own," Zeus replied. "So you were captured by him?"

As they talked, they made their way across the enormous bed. Walking on the lumpy mattress was kind of like walking on quicksand, the way they sank down each time they took a step. But then they'd bob right up again. Poseidon flailed his arms, trying not to lose his balance as they moved.

"Captured by the Cronies," the boy explained as they bobbed up and down. "My twin sister, Artemis, and I were out hunting with bows and arrows when they attacked us. They brought me to Typhon, but I'm not sure where they took my sister. I'm worried about her."

Maybe they took her to King Cronus, and he swallowed her, just like he swallowed the five Olympians before us, Zeus thought. *But then, why didn't he swallow this boy? Isn't he an Olympian too?*

The boy looked so sad, and Demeter gave him a sympathetic smile.

"I'm Demeter, and this is Zeus and Poseidon," she said. "What's your name?"

"Apollo," he answered.

Zzzzzzzzz. Typhon snored again, and this time the wind knocked them all over. They landed flat on their backs, like turtles, with their arms and legs in the air. They struggled to steady themselves in the soft mattress so they could stand back up.

"So what's with Typhon and this wind thing?" Zeus asked as he tried to sit up.

"Typhon's partly giant and partly beast. He's quite dangerous, to say the least," Apollo replied in a singsong voice. Then he got more serious. "He has the power to create huge winds and storms."

Zeus got to his feet first. He made his way to the corner of the bed and looked down at the post they had climbed up earlier.

"It might be harder to climb down this thing

than it was to climb up it," he said as the other three quickly reached him.

"What if we climb down the bedspread instead?" Demeter suggested. "It will be easy to grip, almost like climbing down a rope."

Zeus nodded. "That makes sense."

He grabbed onto the bedspread and slowly made his way over the side of the bed.

"This works great!" he called up to the rest. Poseidon started to climb down too. Apollo stashed his lyre in his sack so he could have both hands free.

Zzzzzzzzzz. Another whirlwind shot from Typhon's nostrils and caused the hanging part of the bedspread to sway back and forth.

"Whoooaaaaa!" Zeus and Poseidon cried out, hanging on tightly. Up top, Demeter and Apollo grabbed the fabric, trying to steady it.

When the bedspread finally stopped moving,

Zeus scrambled down to the floor before the next snore could come. Poseidon jumped down next to him, and together they steadied the fabric as Demeter and then Apollo also climbed down.

Zeus nodded across the room to the crack at the bottom of the door. "That's how we got in," he told Apollo. "Hey, why didn't you try to escape when Typhon was out? Couldn't you squeeze through the crack?"

Apollo shook his head. "Alas, I cannot escape, I fear. This pollen is magic; it keeps me here."

He motioned to the golden grains all over his clothing. Demeter stepped up to get a closer look.

"I thought it was sugar, but it's pollen, all right." she remarked. "That's strange."

Apollo nodded. "The crystals are pollen, this is true. But from which plant, I can't tell you."

"Dude, do you always talk in rhyme?" Poseidon asked.

Apollo shrugged. "Sometimes yes, sometimes no. It helps me think, this I know."

Poseidon shook his head. "'No' and 'know'? That's the best you can do?"

"Hey, give me a break. I'm bummed," Apollo replied in his own defense. "You guys can get out of here, but I'm stuck."

Poseidon held up his trident. "To escape, you just need to get rid of the pollen, right?" he said with a grin. "No problem!"

He held the trident over Apollo's head. Water rained down on the boy from the trident's three prongs. But the pollen didn't wash off. It stuck to Apollo's skin and clothing like glue.

Poseidon frowned. "Why didn't that work?"

Zzzzzzzzzz! A powerful wind whipped across the floor, sending a giant dust bunny rolling toward them like a huge tumbleweed.

"Dodge it!" Zeus yelled. The four Olympians

dove in four different directions. After the dust bunny blew past them, they wearily got back to their feet.

"What are we going to do? We have *got* to get out of here before snore-guy wakes up!" Poseidon exclaimed.

"We can't leave," Demeter said. "Not without Apollo."

Then Zeus remembered something. "And not without the Magic Seeds, either. That's why we climbed the beanstalk all the way up here in the first place."

"Beanstalk?" Apollo asked, puzzled.

"We're all at the top of a giant beanstalk," Zeus explained. "Didn't you know? It started growing just this morning."

Apollo looked thoughtful. "Hmm. Magic Seeds and a beanstalk coming out of nowhere," he muttered. Then his face brightened. "I think

I know these Magic Seeds! So I can give you what you need!"

"Really?" Zeus asked.

"Well, I think so, anyway," Apollo answered. "You see, Typhon has a pouch of these oval-shaped glittering yellow things. He likes to count them just before he goes to bed each night. I thought they were coins at first, and so I asked him why he was counting his money all the time."

"What did he say?" asked Demeter.

"He just laughed," said Apollo. "He said that he wasn't counting money right now, but soon he would be. He said that King Cronus would trade many pouches of gold coins in exchange for this one pouch of oval thingies. When I asked him why, he replied, 'With gold you can *buy* anything, but with what's in the pouch you can *grow* anything.' They must be the Magic Seeds you're looking for!"

"I'm sure glad you didn't sing all of that," Poseidon remarked.

Zeus felt his pulse race with excitement. "You're right!" he told Apollo. "Those must be the Magic Seeds. I bet if one of them dropped out of the pouch and fell to Earth, and that's how the beanstalk grew!"

"So where is the pouch?" Demeter asked, getting excited too.

Apollo pointed to the door, where a gold pouch hung from the doorknob. They all started to make their way across the floor toward it.

Zzzzzzzzz. Typhon snored, and another wind whipped up.

"Quick! Hold hands!" Demeter called out. The four Olympians gripped hands and fought against the wind until they reached the door.

"Trident, long!" Poseidon commanded. The trident's staff grew and grew until it reached the doorknob. Then Poseidon managed to hook the string of the pouch on the prongs of the trident. His tongue stuck out of his mouth as he concentrated on lifting the pouch off the knob and gently lowering it to the floor.

"It's really heavy," Poseidon reported. "And huge." To a giant it would seem a small pouch. But it was actually about the same size as the Olympians.

"How will we get it down the beanstalk?" Demeter wondered aloud. She reached out to touch it. The moment her fingers made contact, the pouch shrunk to the size of a small purse that would fit her! As Zeus wondered how this magic had happened, she quickly hung it around her neck.

"Problem solved," she said with a pleased smile. "Now we just have to figure out how to get Apollo out of here too."

ZZZZZZZZZ. Typhon let out an extra-loud snort this time.

Crash! The wind gust blew the sugar bowl across the table, and it fell to the floor with a clatter. The pollen inside it spilled out. At the same time, the pollen that had been stuck to Apollo fell right off!

"Happier words I have not spoken. It looks like the spell on me has been broken!" Apollo sang, smiling.

But the Olympians couldn't celebrate yet.

"Who goes there?" Typhon bellowed. The crash had awakened him. "Where is my Olympian? I will find youuuuuuu!" He screeched like a wild bird, roared like a lion, and growled like a bear as he slid off his chair. Then he spotted them.

"What treachery is this?" he roared. "Not one of you shall escape!"

"Run!" Zeus cried, and he and the others scurried through the crack at the bottom of the door.

CHAPTER EIGHT

Attack of the Giant Bees

The four Olympians raced through the tall grass, making their way to the beanstalk. Typhon's shadow loomed over them— and then they heard him bellow a command.

"Bees! Attack!" he roared.

"Bees?" Zeus wondered out loud as they ran. He had been raised by a bee named Melissa. So he wasn't afraid of bees like most people were. Melissa had always been nice to him.

"Sizzling stingers! They're enormous!" Poseidon cried out, pointing.

"These bees will harm us, this I fear. We really must get out of here!" sang Apollo.

Zeus looked back as he ran. A small army of furry yellow-and-black bees swarmed toward him. Each bee was as big as one of the Olympians.

The vibrations of their loud humming shook the ground underneath the Olympians' feet. The bees' glossy black eyes seemed to stare right through Zeus. Their twitching jaws and long pink tongues made them look like monsters. A stinger as long and as sharp as a warrior's spear extended from the back of each bee's abdomen.

"Hurry!" Demeter yelled.

"We'll never outrun them," Poseidon countered. He waved his trident. "We should stop and fight."

Zeus's mind raced as he tried to figure out what to do. Poseidon was right—they couldn't outrun the bees. But even though the bees were terrifying, Zeus didn't want to fight them. It wasn't the bees' fault. If Typhon hadn't stirred them up, they probably wouldn't even be chasing the Olympians.

He could see the top of the beanstalk up ahead. They were getting closer. Tendrils snaked out from the stalk, laced with leaves and closed buds.

If only the buds were open, Zeus thought. *There's nothing bees like more than getting pollen from flowers.*

Then he saw Demeter running next to him, and something clicked in his head.

"Demeter! Touch the flower buds!" he yelled.

Demeter looked at him, confused.

"Just do it!" Zeus urged.

The bees were almost on them now, and Poseidon gripped his trident tightly, ready to fight.

"Not yet!" Zeus told him. The urge to keep everyone safe rose strongly in him. After all, Pythia had told him he was the leader of the Olympians. And keeping others safe was what good leaders did! If the Olympians could defeat the bees without fighting them, everyone would win.

Demeter put on a burst of speed and raced up to the nearest tendril of the stalk. She touched the first flower bud she reached, and it opened right up.

"Touch more of them!" yelled Zeus.

Demeter quickly dodged among the vines, opening bud after bud. The bees stopped chasing and zipped right toward the flowers instead. Just as Zeus had hoped they might.

"It's working!" he exclaimed.

Demeter ran back to the three boys and met them as they reached the top of the stalk.

"We made it," Zeus said, breathless. "Now we just need to climb down."

"Roooowwwr!"

A shadow crossed over them. The four Olympians looked up to see Typhon looming near, furiously roaring. Flames shot from his nostrils as he glared at them, snorting in anger. The tangle of serpents he had in place of legs flicked their tongues and wriggled in agitation.

"Bolt, large!" Zeus cried. He nodded at Poseidon, who held up his trident. Then Zeus turned to Demeter and Apollo.

"Go down! We'll hold him off!"

Demeter nodded, but Apollo hesitated. She grabbed him by the hand and tugged. "They've got this," she assured him. Apollo reluctantly followed her.

Zeus and Poseidon tapped Bolt and the trident together just as Typhon reached down to scoop them up in his meaty hand. A bright light flashed from the two magical objects, startling the giant, and he slithered back—but just for a moment.

He lunged forward again, angrier than before.

Splash! Poseidon shot a blast of water right into the giant's eyes.

Zap! Zeus shocked him with a sizzling bolt of energy. Typhon's serpents wiggled wildly, and he began to bleat like an angry goat.

The boys had succeeded in stunning the giant for just a few seconds. It was enough time for them to start scrambling down the beanstalk.

"We're safe! Those snakes can't slither down a beanstalk," Poseidon said as they climbed down the stalk from stem to stem.

"Aiee! Aiee!" The piercing sound of a hawk

filled the air, and a wind whipped up around them.

"Don't forget—he has wings!" Zeus yelled.

Sure enough, Typhon swooped down from the sky, flying right toward them. Zeus zapped him with another jolt from Bolt and sent the giant tumbling backward through the air.

The two boys climbed down a few more feet before Typhon charged them again. This time Poscidon blasted him with a powerful jet of water. Zeus and Poseidon kept moving downward, but Typhon charged at them again. Now he hovered in the air and took a long, deep breath.

"Uh-oh," said Zeus.

WHOOOOSH! A hurricane-strength wind blew from Typhon's powerful lungs and rocked the beanstalk.

Zeus felt his fingers start to slip. He tightened

his grip as his legs were knocked off the vine to wriggle in the air.

Just above him, Poseidon was blown completely off the stalk. Luckily, he grabbed a vine just in time and hung there, swinging.

"That guy really is full of hot air!" Poseidon shouted over the sound of the wind.

Down below, Zeus could see that Apollo and Demeter hadn't reached the ground yet and were barely hanging on too. If Typhon kept this up, they would all be doomed!

WHOOOOSH! Another hurricane wind blew, and the beanstalk swayed violently. Zeus almost lost his grip again.

"Hang on!" he yelled.

CHAPTER NINE

Toppled

The beanstalk rocked back and forth wildly. Zeus's knuckles turned white as he tried to strengthen his grip.

Then a loud, groaning sound filled the air. At first Zeus thought it was one of Typhon's animal sounds. But a second later he realized the sound was coming from the stalk.

Looking down, he saw the stalk's giant roots tear up through the dirt. The wind had pulled the roots right from the ground! His stomach lurched as the giant beanstalk began to topple over.

Down, down, down they went. He closed his eyes as the stalk and the four Olympians along with it plummeted to the ground.

Thump! To Zeus's surprise, he wasn't squashed on impact. He'd fallen on something soft! He opened his eyes. He—along with Poseidon, Demeter, and Apollo—had landed safely on a soft pile of leaves.

"Is everyone okay?" he asked.

The others nodded, looking dazed. Then Hades, Hera, and Hestia ran up.

"I can't believe it! I thought I was going to have to welcome you guys to the Underworld," said Hades.

"We were so scared," Hestia added. "We saw you climbing down, and then that monster appeared."

Zeus sat straight up. "Typhon! We've got to run."

"I wouldn't worry," Hera said, pointing. "The beanstalk whacked him on the head on the way down. He's out cold."

"Typhon is beat! Now, that's really sweet!" Apollo sang out.

Hera made a face. "Um, who's he?" she asked Zeus.

"Apollo," Zeus explained. "He's an Olympian, like us."

"And he really likes to sing and rhyme," Poseidon added.

"Yeah, I noticed," said Hera.

"But what about the Magic Seeds?" asked Hestia. "Did you find those too?"

Demeter climbed down from the leaf pile. She took the pouch from around her neck.

"We did find them," she explained. She spilled

the seeds out into her hand. Each one was about the size of a pumpkin seed. They were golden yellow, and glittered in the sunlight. Quickly she counted them. "There are twenty."

"And Demeter is carrying them because . . ." Hera asked.

"The pouch of seeds was giant-size when we found it," Zeus replied. "But it shrunk when Demeter touched it. Seems like the seeds are connected to her somehow."

Hera's lips got tight, but she said nothing.

"Um, so what do you want to do about the big snaky guy?" Hades asked.

The Olympians cautiously walked up to Typhon's fallen body. The normally slithering snakes were still. Typhon's eyes were closed. But his hairy chest moved up and down as he breathed.

"Ew! He's hideous," said Hera. "Is he a—"

"Creature of Chaos," Zeus finished for her, nodding.

"One that definitely needs to be locked up in Tartarus in the Underworld," Hades put in. "He can keep the Titans we've already sent there company."

"We'd better do it soon," Poseidon remarked. "Because I think he's waking up."

Typhon's eyelids were starting to flutter. His serpent legs were stirring.

"I can't just send a hurricane-blasting giant down to the Underworld," Hades said. "He could wind up freeing the Titans."

"Anyone have some giant handcuffs?" Poseidon asked. "Or a muzzle?"

"Why not try a Magic Seed? It might be exactly what you need," Apollo suggested.

"What can the seeds do? Cover him with flowers?" Hera scoffed.

Demeter looked down at her pouch. "If Apollo heard Typhon right, the seeds can grow anything," she said. "Bet they could grow vines strong enough to hold a giant. Even one this big!"

"Do it!" Zeus urged.

But Demeter frowned. "Pythia said that the seeds would help us regrow the land. I don't want to waste even one."

Typhon's snakes opened their eyes. Their red tongues flicked out.

"When Typhon wakes up and gets going again, there won't *be* any more land," Poseidon pointed out.

Hera looked at her friend. "It's just one seed. I think you should do it."

Demeter nodded. She plucked one of the seeds from the pouch. Then she got as close to Typhon as she could and planted it in the ground.

Immediately something burst from the dirt. But it wasn't a vine. It was a strong metal chain!

"Wow, those are Magic Seeds, all right!" Poseidon exclaimed.

More and more metal chains snaked from the seed, slipping over and under Typhon. Within seconds the chains completely contained him.

"Nice," Hades said. "Now let me do my thing."

He clapped his hands. "Chariot, appear!"

Typhon's eyes flew open when he heard the clap. He glanced down at the chains binding him.

"Rawwwwr!" His lion roar shook the fallen beanstalk as he struggled to break through the chains.

"Um, Hades?" Poseidon asked nervously. But just then . . .

Boom! A huge hole opened up right near Typhon. A chariot drawn by four black horses emerged from the hole.

"Take this beast to Tartarus!" Hades commanded.

"Nooooo!" Typhon wailed as the chariot dragged him into the hole.

Then the hole closed up. Poseidon gazed worriedly at the broken earth.

"I sure hope those chains can hold him," he said.

"Don't worry," Hades said with a grin. "Cerberus and the Furies will be waiting for them."

Zeus nodded. Cerberus was Hades's three-headed dragon dog. And the Furies were three fierce flying guardians of the Underworld. They worked for Hades now, but the Olympians had faced them when they hadn't been so friendly. All together, they would be every bit a match for Typhon!

"So what do we do now?" Poseidon wondered aloud.

Just as he finished speaking, a cloud of glittery mist appeared before the Olympians. A face framed by long black hair appeared in the mist.

Apollo smiled. "Pythia!" he exclaimed.

CHAPTER TEN

Brothers and Sisters?

Zeus was confused. "You know Pythia?" he asked Apollo.

"Sure," Apollo replied. He nodded to the oracle's face in the mist. "So, are your spectacles still fogging up?"

"As a matter of fact, they are," Pythia replied. She took off her glasses to polish them. "Are you keeping up with lyre practice?"

"I try to play, almost every day," he sang in

reply. Then his smile faded. "Pythia, do you know where Artemis is?"

"Who's Artemis?" Hera interrupted.

"My twin sister," Apollo explained. "She was captured by the Cronies at the same time I was."

"I see that she is safe, but her location is unclear to me," the oracle answered. "Although I fear there are bubbles brewing."

"Bubbles?" Poseidon asked hopefully.

He must be missing the sea, thought Zeus.

Pythia polished her glasses again. "Oh dear. I meant 'troubles.' There are troubles brewing."

Apollo's face darkened. "Then I've got to find her."

"You will, in time," Pythia said. "But for now I must congratulate all of you. You have found the Magic Seeds."

Demeter stepped forward. "They're in this pouch. There were twenty, but I had to use one to imprison Typhon. We thought it would grow vines, but instead metal chains grew, right from the ground."

Pythia nodded. "Yes, the seeds can transform into anything. And it is right that they are in your care, Demeter. But I warn you not to use the seeds for silly purposes. Plant one in every village you reach. From each seed many different kinds of crops will grow."

Demeter gazed at the pouch of Magic Seeds in new wonder. "I promise, I will."

"And now begins a new quest," Pythia said. "You must find the aegis. It's a shield that one wears over a tunic. A hundred tassels of pure gold hang from it."

"Where will we find it?" Zeus asked.

"You must travel to the shores of Lake Stymphalia, near Corinth," she replied. "But obtaining the aegis will not be easy. You must win it through battle."

"So what else is new?" Poseidon mumbled.

"Well, good luck, guys," Apollo told the others. "I'm off to find Artemis."

"Apollo, no!" Pythia warned. "All of the Olympians must stay together. You must work as a team. That is the only way you will ever defeat the dark forces that are gathering."

Apollo sighed. "Whatever you say, Pyth."

Zeus felt bad for him. He kind of knew how Apollo must be feeling. Ever since his journey had begun, he'd wanted to find his mother. But Pythia always had a new quest for them. She'd told him to wait.

"So I guess I can't look for my mother yet?" Zeus asked sadly. "Do you remember what her name is this time? Rhea? Lea? Mia?"

"I'm certain that it's Rhea," Pythia answered as her image began to flicker in the mist.

"That's weird," Poseidon said slowly. "I never

told you guys this before, but Oceanus said *my* mother's name is Rhea."

Pythia's image brightened again for a moment, and she cocked her head. "Well, of course it is," she said. "Rhea bore six of you Olympians. All except Apollo. Though, of course, there are more of you, as yet undiscovered."

The Olympians gaped at her in surprise as her image began to fade again. Then suddenly the mist disappeared completely, and Pythia with it.

"So except for Apollo we're all brothers and sisters?" Zeus said, staring around at the others. His eyes settled on Hera. "Did you know this? Just like you knew I was an Olympian but didn't tell me for a long time?"

For a moment Hera's eyes slid away from his. But when she looked back at him, she said, "To tell the truth, I kind of guessed it. But I didn't know for sure. I promise."

"I never knew my mother, or her name," Hades added.

"Me neither," said Hestia.

"Or me," Demeter chimed in.

"I always thought I was an only child," said Zeus, feeling dazed.

Apollo patted him on the back. "Congratulations. Looks like you've got more siblings than you can shake a stick at—or a thunderbolt, anyway."

"Looks like you, me, and Hades are bros, Zeus," Poseidon said. "High-five!"

Still in a daze, Zeus slapped Poseidon's hand, and then Hades's hand too. He had grown up all alone, raised by a bee and a goat and a nymph. He'd thought he had no family. And now he had five brothers and sisters?

"Yeah, we're all one big happy family," Hera said, rolling her eyes. "So which way now, Shock Boy?"

Zeus tried to get used to the idea that she was his sister. Just like Demeter and Hestia! And he knew how bad Hera must feel about not having a magical object. Besides Apollo, Hera was the only one without a magical object now. At least Apollo had his lyre. Hera had nothing.

Zeus slipped the cord from around his neck. "Here, why don't you ask Chip," he said. "You can wear him if you want."

Hera's face softened. "Sure, thanks."

She slipped Chip over her neck and then held the amulet in her palm. "Okay, Chip. Which way to Corinth?"

An arrow appeared on Chip's surface. It spun around, and then it stopped, pointing northeast.

"Northeast it is," Hera said. "To Corinth!"

Leaving the fallen beanstalk behind, they started toward the nearest road.

"Isn't it amazing that six of us are related?"

said Hades as he walked alongside Zeus. "I mean, we're all so different."

"That's for sure," said Poseidon.

Hestia was playing with her torch, twirling it like a baton. She glanced over at Apollo. "Even if you're not our brother, we're all Olympians, right?"

"Right!" six voices chorused in reply.

Another thought occurred to Zeus. "So does anyone know who our father is?"

Everyone shook their head.

"I guess it's a mystery," said Demeter. "For now, anyway."

As they walked, Apollo strummed on his lyre and sang a song.

"Some brave Olympians climbed the beanstalk
And fought a giant who roars like a beast.
They freed the captive and got Magic Seeds,
And now we're all headed to the northeast."

Zeus shaded his eyes against the sun to see what the land ahead looked like. Something glinted in the sky in the distance. Squinting, he realized it was a flock of birds. They slowly flew in a circle. When the sun hit them, they sparkled. Huh? What kind of feathers sparkled?

"Those birds sure look weird," he said, a little nervously.

"Worried they'll peck your eyes out?" Hera teased.

"No, but I'm just saying, they're shiny," Zeus replied. "Almost like they're made of . . . metal, or something."

He turned to Poseidon, who was making water bubbles with his trident. Demeter giggled as she tried to catch them as they floated in the air.

"Do you see what I mean?" Zeus asked.

Poseidon shrugged. "We just fought a half-dragon, half-giant with snakes for legs. I'm not worried about some shiny birds."

"Poseidon's right. We should have a little fun while we can," Hestia said, tossing her flaming baton into the air.

Hades grinned. "Okay, then, here's a joke. Why do hummingbirds hum?" he asked.

"I don't know," said Hera.

"Because they don't know the words!" he replied, cracking himself up.

Hera groaned and shook her head.

Zeus laughed at Hades's joke, but then he glanced up at the birds again. Was he the only one who was worried about them? Or about what troubles they might find in Corinth? As the Olympians headed toward the huge flock of birds, Zeus wished he could shake the bad feeling he had.

The feeling that there was going to be a *peck* of bird-pecking trouble up ahead!